HENRY
the
Brave Little Tractor

Written by:
Morris F. Garcia

Illustrated by: Ernie (HERGIE) Hergenroeder

This book dedicated to:
KIM
4-14-1966 • 3-9-1992

The story "HENRY The Brave Little Tractor" is an imprint of Bar 94 Publishing Inc.
Published by: Bar 94 Publishing Inc.
1959 Gateway Blvd., Suite 102
Fresno, CA 93727
Copyright © 2012 Morris F. Garcia
Fresno, California
All rights reserved.
Printed in Hong Kong
10 9 8 7 6 5 4 3 2 1

Library of Congress Control Number: 2012908533
Morris F. Garcia
The story of "HENRY The Brave Little Tractor" written by Morris F. Garcia
Illustrated by Ernie "Hergie" Hergenroeder
Summary: "HENRY The Brave Little Tractor", is the story of a 2N Ford tractor named Henry.
His adventures from 1942 to today. His brave service to country, community and his owners.
ISBN: 978-0-9855554-0-5 (Hardcover)
Copyright to include all characters, design & story concept.

In early 1942 the last Ford Tractor was built in Richmond, California. World War II was well underway, and the United States needed the factory to build tanks and jeeps for the war effort. The last little tractors built were painted two tone red and gray because of a paint shortage. Tomorrow this one is scheduled to ship to a tractor dealer in Escalon, California.

1

2 Farmers were in need of tractors because none would be built after 1942. The little tractor was loaded onto a train and was to be delivered to Bob's Tractor Store in Escalon, California. Surely there will be a farmer there that will buy this little tractor with its very odd two tone paint job.

The little tractor arrived at Bob's Tractor Store on a warm spring day under a bright blue sky. But as expected, the farmers objected to the odd two tone paint job. The little tractor would blink his lights at passers-by, but no one was interested in looking. Then, one day . . .

3

4 . . . A Navy Seabee on leave, visiting his family, walked into Bob's Tractor Store. Seabee Lee saw the little tractor and thought that the Seabees could use a tractor like this one. We can haul supplies for the U.S. Marines in the South Pacific with it. "I'll buy this tractor if you can have it ready to go in a week," said Seabee Lee. "You have just bought a tractor," said dealer Bob.

The week passed and Seabee Lee took his new little tractor to the Port of Stockton to ship over seas. It was a little scary being loaded onto the big, tall ship with a crane. Seabee Lee shouted to the little tractor, "Way to go Henry!" Seabee Lee named him Henry after his creator, Henry Ford. "Is that my name," thought Henry? "I LIKE IT!"

5

6 Seabee Lee and Henry sailed across the Pacific Ocean with the U.S. Marines. When they arrived at the islands, the war was in full action. Seabee Lee shouted, " Man your battle stations men, this looks like war!" Henry thought, "it looks like time to get to work". The loud explosions and the airplanes that were flying overhead were very scary!

The Navy Seabees followed the Marines onto the island and built air fields and supply depots. Henry hauled bombs and bullets to the Marines that were fighting on the island. Henry worked day and night for three years and suffered bullet holes in his hood during battle. He was awarded the purple heart and promoted to Seabee Sergeant. Henry became a hero that day.

7

8   When the war came to an end in 1945, much of the equipment and supplies were to be left on the island. The soldiers began boarding the ships for their voyage back home to the United States. Henry was parked with the discarded equipment. "OH, NO!" thought Henry. "I want to go home too." He began blinking his lights to draw attention, but the soldiers kept marching by.

Then all of a sudden Seabee Lee was standing right in front of Henry. "What are you doing here, Henry?" said Seabee Lee. I'm not going to leave you here; I have plenty of room on my ship for you ." Seabee Lee started Henry's motor and took him down to the docks to go home. Henry was so happy. "YEA, I'm going home!" thought Henry.

9

10 The ship arrived at the Port of Stockton in California, after a long and exciting journey across the Pacific Ocean. Seabee Lee had mailed a letter to Bob's Tractor Store to meet Henry and him at the port. Bob was there with his truck ready to take Henry back to Escalon for a new paint job and some fixing up. "Take care of Henry," said Seabee Lee. "He's a hero you know!"

Bob brought Henry back to his tractor store. The men sanded and scraped the rust and grime off of Henry. They repaired the motor with new parts and gave him a new coat of paint. They put on new tires, seat and steering wheel. Farmers were in need of new tractors after the four years of war. "Wow, Henry looks as good as he did when he was a new tractor," said Bob.

11

12 Henry was placed in the store window with a sign announcing "NEW TRACTOR SALE". That day farmer Don was driving by and spotted the sign. Farmer Don stopped and looked at this new little tractor. "I think that he'll be perfect to work in my apricot orchard," thought Don. Don and Bob made a deal, and soon Henry was on a truck headed for Don's Apricot Farm.

Henry spent many days in the apricot orchards at farmer Don's. He was so glad to be doing the work he was created to do. Henry lived in Patterson, California, the apricot capital of the world. Working with farmer Don and all his helpers was so peaceful, picking and preparing the apricots to be shipped all over the world.

13

14 One day farmer Don brought home a BIG, new tractor. "OH, NO! What's happening," thought
Henry.   Farmer Don washed Henry and placed him by the barn with a big sign. Henry was
no longer needed because the new tractor was less expensive to operate. Henry was sad
because he knew it was time to move again. "What's going to happen to me now," he thought.

During the next week many people came by to look at Henry. One man almost bought him to take him to the scrap iron yard to be recycled. Then on a sunny day a man named Mister Morris came by and looked at Henry. He kicked the tires, looked at his motor and started it. "Sounds good," said Mister Morris. "I'll take him." Soon Henry was loaded on a truck.

15

16 The next day Henry was put in Mister Morris' shop, and two men began taking the parts off of him. "OH, NO! What are they doing to me?" thought Henry. The men sanded and scraped the rust and dirt. "We'll make him new again. I have an idea for a new seat on the back that my grandchildren can ride on," said Grandpa Morris.

Grandpa Morris worked all night building a special surprise for his grandchildren. He made a bench large enough for all of them to ride on the back of Henry. Grandpa Morris restored Henry to his original condition. Henry thought, "Maybe I will be working in the orchards again. I feel so happy that Grandpa Morris bought me." Finally, all the work was complete.

17

18 Henry could not wait any longer. He wanted to see what Grandpa Morris had built on him.
There was a mirror in the back of the shop. Grandpa Morris pulled it out so Henry could see.
"WOW, I look as good as I did when I was born in 1942," thought Henry! "You're now ready
for the parade I have entered you in, Henry," said Grandpa Morris.

The day arrived for Grandpa Morris to get ready for the parade. Everyone was so excited to climb onto Henry and the special seat that Grandpa Morris built. Alexis, Tevin, Mikalya, Malia and Grandma Sharon got seated and then Grandpa Morris took the driver's seat. "Is everyone ready? OK, let's go and get in line for the parade," said Grandpa Morris.

19

20 Grandpa Morris drove Henry to where the parade begins. They got in line behind the high school marching band and in front of the clowns in their funny cars. There were people already standing and sitting, waiting for the parade to begin. Henry was very nervous, this wasn't like the quiet orchards at farmer Don's. Then the music started and it was time to go.

The parade was underway and Grandpa Morris drove slowly down the main street. Henry was blinking his lights while the crowd was cheering and shouting. All of a sudden, Henry saw Seabee Lee waving from the crowd. Henry was so happy to see his old war buddy, but why was he at this parade? Grandpa Morris and Grandma Sharon were waving to Seabee Lee. "Do they know Seabee Lee?"

When Henry got to the end of the parade, there stood Seabee Lee with a big smile on his face. Grandpa Morris and Grandma Sharon jumped down and greeted Seabee Lee with a big hug. "What a great surprise," thought Henry. Everyone was so happy to see each other, and so was the littlest tractor from 1942, Henry the Seabee war hero.

22

Grandpa Morris, Seabee Lee and Henry enjoyed giving the neighborhood children and their friends rides in the warm California sun. Lois and Pat, Henry's good friends came by often to see all the fun they were having. If you are ever at a special event and see Henry and Grandpa Morris there, don't forget to ask if you can have a ride too!

23

Farmer
DON

Grandpa
MORRIS

Seabee
LEE

Tractor Dealer
BOB

Seabee LEE and young Grandpa MORRIS

Grandpa Morris' four granddaughters, (L to R) Malia, Tevin, Alexis & Mikalya